Best Friend Stories

True Stories About Dogs

A Dolch Classic Basic Reading Book

by Edward W. Dolch and Marguerite P. Dolch

illustrated by Meryl Henderson

The Basic Reading Books

The Basic Reading Books are fun reading books that fill the need for easy-to-read stories for the primary grades. The interest appeal of these folktales and legends will encourage independent reading at the early reading levels.

The stories focus on the 95 Common Nouns and the Dolch 220 Basic Sight Vocabulary. Beyond these simple lists, the books use about two or three new words per page.

This series was prepared under the direction and supervision of Edward W. Dolch, Ph.D.

This revision was prepared under the direction and supervision of Eleanor Dolch LaRoy and the Dolch Family Trust.

SRA/McGraw-Hill

*A Division of The **McGraw·Hill** Companies*

Send all inquires to:
SRA/McGraw-Hill
8787 Orion Place
Columbus, OH 43240-4027

ISBN 0-02-830818-2

3 4 5 6 7 8 9 0 QST 04 03

Table of Contents

Golden Queen

Bob lived on a big farm. There were no children to play with. But Bob had a pet, big dog called Golden Queen.

Bob and Golden Queen liked living on a farm. They played together every day. They walked over the fields and in the woods. Once, when Bob was lost in a corn field, and the sun went down, Golden Queen found the way out.

Everyone has to learn to work on a big farm. Bob helped his father with the work. He learned to help with the corn. He learned to look after the chickens and the sheep and the cows. He learned always to shut the gate to the pasture where Tony, the big, black bull, lived. Tony was very big. He had big horns, and you could never tell what he would do.

Golden Queen learned to work on the farm, too. She followed Bob. She learned not to walk on the little corn when it first came up. She learned to keep the cats away from the little chickens.

Golden Queen could tell which sheep was the leader. All of the sheep would follow the leader. Golden Queen could take the sheep from the barn to the pasture, and not one sheep would be lost.

Every day Golden Queen would help Bob bring the cows in from the pasture to the milking barn where Father milked them. Some of the cows would be far away in the pasture when it was time for them to be milked. Golden Queen would run after them. She would bark at them. Then, the cows would go to the milking barn.

But Golden Queen would not have anything to do with Tony, the big black bull with the horns. When Tony saw Golden Queen in his pasture, he would put his head down and run after the big dog. Golden Queen would run as fast as she could, because Tony could kill a dog or a person with his big horns.

One day, after Bob had put the cows in the milking barn, he saw that the gate to Tony's pasture was open. He went to shut it, because his father had always said that the gate to the pasture where Tony lived must always be shut. Bob saw that he had to go into the pasture to pull the gate shut.

Tony, the big, black bull, saw Bob. He did not want Bob in his pasture. He put his head down. He ran at Bob. Golden Queen saw that Tony would hurt Bob with his big horns.

Bob was afraid. He heard Tony coming at him. He jumped away, but he fell as he did so. Tony was running right at Bob. Golden Queen saw that she must stop Tony. So she jumped at Tony's legs and bit them again and again.

Tony stopped. His legs hurt very much. He wanted to kill that dog that was hurting his legs. So, he tried to get at Golden Queen.

The dog bit the bull again and again. Then, Golden Queen jumped away before Tony could get her. The big bull

could not get at Golden Queen with his horns. The big bull gave up and ran away as fast as he could go.

Golden Queen ran back to Bob to see whether he was all right. Father, who had been in the milking barn, came running. He had a big stick, but he did not have to use it. He took Bob into the house to see whether he was all right, because Bob had hurt his leg when he fell down. Golden Queen walked right into the house, too.

Bob told Mother and Father what Golden Queen had done. Father and Mother both said that if it had not been for Golden Queen, Tony would have killed Bob.

Golden Queen lived to be a very old dog. When Father or Mother looked at her, they always wanted to thank her for what she had done when Tony, the big black bull, had tried to kill Bob.

Bunny and Bunco

Bunny was a little girl. And Bunco was her dog. Every day you could see Bunny and Bunco out walking. Sometimes they would be going to the store to get some bread for Mother. Sometimes they would just be taking a walk together.

Bunco always took very good care of Bunny. He was careful when they came to streets. Bunny must not get hurt.

Bunny got Bunco as puppy when Daddy went away to war.

"The puppy's name is 'Bunco'," said Daddy. "Take good care of this puppy and he will take care of you."

Mother was happy to have Bunco, too, because it was very lonesome without Daddy.

Bunco grew to be a big brown dog. He came to know that he was to look after Mother and Bunny.

At first Bunco barked and barked at the mailman. But he learned that Mother was very happy to see the mailman. She would laugh when the mailman had a letter from Daddy.

Then, Bunco barked and barked at the milkman. But he soon learned that the milkman came every day with milk. Bunny would give him some milk. And Bunco liked milk.

But there was one man who did not come every day. Mother told Bunco that this man was all right. This man would come right into the house. He looked at something and put something in a book that he carried. Bunco did not know what to make of this man. He barked and barked and barked at him.

The man only laughed and said, "You are a good watchdog."

"Bunco is the best watchdog that ever lived," said Bunny. "He looks after Mother, and he looks after me while Daddy is away at the war."

As Bunco grew, he learned not to bark at friends.

When someone came to the house, Mother would say, "Bunco, this is one of my friends."

And Bunco would know that he was not to bark. He never barked at the children that Bunny played with. They all loved Bunco, and they had many good times playing together.

But one night Bunco was asleep in the living room where Mother let him have his bed. Mother and Bunny were asleep in their bedrooms. In his sleep, Bunco heard a noise. Bunco woke up. He heard someone coming up the walk to the door. He went to the door and gave a little bark. He knew that someone was by the door. But that someone was very quiet.

Then, Bunco heard someone walking outside around the house. Then, he heard someone at the backdoor. Bunco ran to the backdoor. Someone tried to open the backdoor. Bunco jumped at the door and barked.

This was no friend. Friends came in the daytime. This was someone who was trying to get into the house in the night.

Bunco was not going to let anyone get into the house and hurt Mother and Bunny.

Then, he heard a noise at a window. Someone was trying to open a window. Bunco ran and jumped up at the window. He could see a man. And this man was no friend.

The man went away from the window. Bunco heard him walking around the house. Then, Bunco heard the doorbell ring. Bunco ran to the door and barked.

Pretty soon Mother came out of the bedroom looking very sleepy. And Bunny came out of her room looking very sleepy, too.

"Bunco, Bunco," said Mother. "Who is at the door at this time of the night?"

Bunco barked and barked. He tried to tell her that a man wanted to get into the house.

Mother looked out the window. Then, she opened the door. Bunco tried to jump at the man. But Mother put her arms around the man and started to laugh and cry all at once. Bunny jumped up and down and cried, "Daddy, Daddy, Daddy."

Bunco had not seen Daddy for over a year. But he saw that this man must be a friend because Bunny and Mother were so happy to see him.

"You have a good watchdog," said Daddy. "I could not get into my own house."

"You should not come in the night without letting us know," said Mother.

"I got a ride on an airplane, and I did not have time to let you know," said Father. "I wanted to surprise you."

"You did surprise us. But you forgot about Bunco," said Bunny. "You forgot that Bunco was looking after Mother and me when you were away at war."

Everyone was so happy. Now Bunco did not want to bark at all. He just sat and wagged his tail.

Red Lady

Mrs. Curtis did not like dogs. And so when Mr. Curtis came home with Red Lady, she was not very happy about it.

"Little Harry is growing up, and he should have a dog," said Mr. Curtis.

"Little Harry is only three," said Mrs. Curtis. "What would he want with a big dog?"

"Red Lady and Little Harry can grow up together," said Mr. Curtis. "They will be friends. I think children should have a dog for a friend."

"Well," said Mrs. Curtis, "you will have to make a doghouse. Red Lady will have to live in the backyard. I cannot have a big dog in the house."

In the day Red Lady played with Little Harry on the grass in the backyard. They played ball. But never once did Red Lady try to bite Little Harry. And when Little Harry went to sleep in the grass, Red Lady went to sleep at his feet. But at night when Mrs. Curtis put Little Harry to bed, Red Lady went to sleep in the doghouse out in the backyard.

One day Mr. Curtis came home very happy.

"In three days we can go on our vacation," he said.

"Good," said Mrs. Curtis. "Are we going to the lake again?"

"Yes," said Mr. Curtis. "I have taken a house right by the lake."

"Who will look after Red Lady for us when we are away?" asked Mrs. Curtis.

"We shall take Red Lady with us," said Mr. Curtis.

"I don't think that I will like to have Red Lady on our vacation," said Mrs. Curtis.

"Red Lady will play with Little Harry. She will help look after him," said Mr. Curtis.

The day came for Mr. and Mrs. Curtis and Little Harry to drive to the lake. Red Lady watched everything. She knew Little Harry was going away. Red Lady was very unhappy. She went out in the backyard and went into the doghouse. Then, she heard Mr. Curtis calling, "Red Lady, Red Lady, come here."

Red Lady ran around the house, her head up and her tail wagging.

Mr. Curtis opened the door to the car. "Get in, Red Lady," he said. "You are going on a vacation, too."

Red Lady was a very happy dog. She and Little Harry sat together in the car. Pretty soon Red Lady went to sleep. It was a long ride to the lake. And Little Harry went to sleep, too, with his head on Red Lady.

Little Harry and Red Lady played together at the lake. They played in the woods. And they played in the water. And always Red Lady watched Little Harry so that he would not get hurt.

Right in front of the house at the lake was a dock that went out into the deep water. Mr. Curtis got into the boat at the dock and went fishing. Mrs. Curtis sat in a chair to watch Mr. Curtis out on the lake.

Little Harry and Red Lady were playing together. They were playing a game of "Try to find me." Little Harry would go behind a tree, and then Red Lady would run and find him. The little boy and the big red dog thought that "Try to find me" was a good game.

While they were playing the game, Mrs. Curtis went in the house to get something.

Then Little Harry got tired of playing "Try to find me." He wanted to play on the dock. He ran down to the water and out onto the dock. Red Lady ran right after him, because she knew that Little Harry must not run out onto the dock. Red Lady barked and barked. Little Harry ran right on. Then, he slipped on the dock and fell right into the water.

At once Red Lady jumped into the water. She took hold of Little Harry to keep his head out of the water. Then, she started to swim.

Mrs. Curtis heard Red Lady barking. She came out of the house. Mrs. Curtis looked around, and she did not see Little Harry or Red Lady. Then, Mrs. Curtis ran to the dock as fast as she could run.

Mrs. Curtis saw Red Lady swimming with Little Harry. The dog was bringing the little boy out of the water.

Mr. Curtis had come back from the lake when he saw Little Harry fall off the dock. He helped Red Lady get Little Harry out of the water. He took up the little boy in his arms. Mrs. Curtis was laughing and crying at the same time. She had the great big, wet dog in her arms, and she was as wet as Little Harry. Red Lady was trying to tell her that everything was all right.

"I am so happy that Red Lady came with us on our vacation," said Mrs. Curtis.

From that time on, Red Lady never went to sleep in a doghouse again. She always went to sleep right by Little Harry's bed. And Red Lady was very happy.

Duke and Queenie

Duke was a very big dog. He lived with Mr. Byron in a beautiful house on a farm. And Duke tried to look after everything about the beautiful house. He tried to look after everything on the farm, too. He would walk around looking to see that all the chickens were in the chicken yard and that all the horses were in the field. He would watch anyone who came to the house to see whether they were friends. He was such a big dog that one growl would make anyone who was not a friend go away.

One day, Mrs. Byron went to see a friend, and when she came back, she had with her a little dog named Queenie. How Mr. Byron laughed when he saw Queenie, because Queenie was not much bigger than Mr. Byron's two hands. Queenie was a happy little dog. She ran around the house putting her nose into everything. Everyone loved Queenie. That is, everyone but Duke.

At first, Duke would not look at Queenie. Queenie would bark her little bark and play around Duke's big feet. She would sometimes try to bite him. But Duke would not look at Queenie. Then, Queenie would bark and bark. But she could not get Duke to look at her. Duke would get tired of all this noise at his feet. Then, he would growl. Queenie would run away. Maybe she was afraid, or maybe she was just playing.

Mrs. Byron was afraid that Duke would hurt Queenie. Mr. Byron knew that Duke would not hurt anything that was in the house or the yard. But, Mr. Byron would say to Mrs. Byron, "Yes, you are going to have to be careful of Queenie. One of these days Duke will take a big bite, and there will be no Queenie."

Then, one day Mr. and Mrs. Byron wanted to take a vacation. They were going to be away a long time. Some friends were coming to live in their beautiful house. These friends said that they could take care of Queenie. But, they were afraid of Duke, because he was a very big dog. And so Mr. Byron took Duke to some friends of his, Mr. and Mrs. Adams, who lived down the road.

Duke was very unhappy in his new home. Mr. Adams tied Duke so that he would not run away. All day Duke lay with his head on his paws. When Mrs. Adams gave Duke a dish of food, Duke would not eat. One day Mrs. Adams did not tie him and tried to get him to play with a stick. But Duke just lay with his head on his paws and would not play.

Just then Mrs. Adams was called into the house. At once Duke jumped up and ran away.

Mr. and Mrs. Adams could not find Duke. They got into their car and went to Mr. Byron's house. Queenie was happy to see them. She jumped all about and barked and barked her little bark. But no one had seen Duke.

Mr. and Mrs. Adams did not know what to do. They had told Mr. Byron that they would take good care of Duke.

In the morning Mr. and Mrs. Adams went back to Mr. Byron's house again to see whether Duke had come back. But this time there was no Queenie to bark at them. And no one had seen Duke. Everyone said that Queenie and Duke had both run away.

Two days went by. Then, as Mrs. Adams went out to get the mail from the mail box, she saw a very big dog coming down the road. It was Duke. He was carrying Queenie in his teeth just like a mother cat carries her kitten.

Duke put Queenie down at Mrs. Adams' feet. Then, he showed in every way that he could that he wanted Queenie to be with him. He showed Queenie his water dish and his bed. He ran to Mrs. Adams again and looked up at her as much as to say, "Please give us something to eat."

Mrs. Adams liked dogs, and she could tell what Duke wanted to say. She gave the dogs a dish of food. She found a small box for Queenie to sleep in. And Duke was happy.

Then, Mrs. Adams wrote a letter to Mrs. Byron and told her about Duke and Queenie. She said that she would keep both of the dogs at her house, because Duke would not eat if Queenie was not with him.

From that time on Duke and Queenie were always together. They played together, and they went to sleep together. It was a funny thing to see a very big dog trying to play with a very little dog.

Queenie learned to ride on Duke's back. But when Duke wanted to get Queenie somewhere, he would take her in his teeth and carry her like a mother cat carries a kitten. And never once did Duke hurt Queenie in any way.

Teddy

When Teddy went to his new home, all the children were fast asleep. The children were not little boys and girls. They were big boys and girls going to school. But they all loved dogs. It was night time, but Mother got them all up, because she knew that they would want to see the new puppy.

Teddy was very little. He was like a round ball, and he had beautiful red hair. He had big brown eyes. When Teddy started to play, the brown eyes were full of fun.

The children loved Teddy right away. They said he was the most beautiful little puppy they had ever seen. Teddy knew that he would like this new home. Teddy loved all the children. But he loved the two boys, Edward and John, the best. That first night, he went to sleep in John's arms.

All the family were afraid that Teddy would get lost. Father went to the store and got Teddy a little collar and a long leash. The girls put the collar on Teddy. They hooked the leash to the collar. Then they took Teddy for a walk.

Teddy had a good time on his first walk in the city.

But Teddy had to learn many new things on his first walk in the city. Teddy had to learn that little puppies must not go into the street. In the city, the street is full of cars that could hurt little puppies. Teddy had to learn that he must follow just the one who was taking him for a walk. Teddy did his best to please. But one thing Teddy did not learn that first day. And that was to come when his name was called. When he lived with his mother in the barn on the farm no one had ever called him "Teddy." He did not know that "Teddy" was the new name John had given him.

When Teddy got home from his first walk, he was a very tired little puppy. He went to sleep in his new bed that Edward and John had made out of a box. After a long time he woke up. He cried a little, because at first he did not know where he was. No one came to him, and so he cried again. But no one came. Then, he cried and cried. He heard a door open. Edward said, "Are you a lonesome little puppy, because the family is not at home?"

Teddy jumped and jumped. He barked his baby bark. He was so happy to see Edward.

Edward sat down on the floor and played with Teddy. Then, he said, "Little puppy, I think that you want some milk." Edward got some milk and warmed it. He put a paper on the floor. And he put a dish of milk on the paper. Teddy liked the warm milk very much.

"And now, Teddy," said Edward, "I will take you for a walk. I will take you to the park where you can run around on the green grass."

Edward got the leash and hooked it onto Teddy's collar. He started up the street with the little puppy following him.

They walked and they walked. Pretty soon they came to a park. There were trees and beautiful green grass all around. Teddy was very happy. This was just like his old home on the farm. He wanted to run and run and run. But he could not run far. The leash made him fall over on his little nose. And so Edward took the leash from Teddy's collar.

Teddy was just as happy as a little puppy could be. He ran and ran with his nose down, smelling the good smells in the grass. Before long Teddy was over the hill. Edward could not see him.

Edward called, "Teddy, Teddy, come here, Teddy, Teddy." But Teddy did not know his name. He just ran on and on and smelled the good smells in the grass.

But the sun was going down, and it was getting dark. Teddy did not come when he was called. Edward could not see the red puppy.

Soon it was dark in the park. Edward called and called, "Teddy." Edward knew that he must find the puppy. Who would help him find Teddy?

At last Edward went to the police station and told the police how he had lost a very little puppy with red hair in the park. Would the police please help him to find the puppy? He told the police just what Teddy looked like and just how big he was. The police said that all of the police cars would look out for a little puppy with red hair.

Then, Edward went to the radio station and talked to the man there. He told him that a little red puppy had been lost in the park. And the man at the radio station told everyone over the radio to look out for a little red puppy that was lost.

That was all Edward could think of to do to find the lost puppy. It was very dark, and he must go home and tell the family about Teddy.

The family was afraid that they would never see their little red puppy again.

Father called up the police station. But no one had heard that a lost red puppy had been found. Mother called the radio station. But no one had told the radio station that a lost red puppy had been found. The family went to bed. And some of them cried a little before they went to sleep.

Now what did the little red puppy do in the park?

The little red puppy ran and ran and smelled and smelled. He got very tired. And so he just went to sleep under a tree. When he woke up, it was very dark. Teddy cried a little, because he was lonesome. It was very dark, and he could not see anything. But he could smell. Teddy could smell where he had run around in the grass. Pretty soon he smelled another smell. He could smell where Edward had been walking.

Edward had given Teddy some warm milk. Teddy wanted some more warm milk. He wanted to find Edward. Smelling every bit of the way, Teddy followed Edward. It took a long, long time for the little puppy to smell his way back to his new home. But after a long time, he got to the house. It was the right house, because his nose told him that Edward had gone in the door. Teddy barked his baby bark and cried and cried. He cried and cried again and again.

Edward had not been sleeping very well. He woke up, and he heard a puppy crying. Then, he heard a little puppy crying again and again.

Edward jumped out of bed and ran to the door. When he opened the door, there was a tired, little red puppy. He looked up at Edward as if to say, "Where have you been? Why did it take you so long to come and open this door and let me in?"

Teddy lived to be an old, old dog. He loved his family very much. But he loved the boys, John and Edward, the best of all.

Shrdlu

Shrdlu is a very funny name for a dog. And I don't think there has ever before been a dog named Shrdlu. This is how Shrdlu got her name.

It was a cold day. The cold wind blew the snow up and down the streets of the town. An unhappy-looking dog came into the office of the newspaper. She was a friendly dog, and the people in the office liked her. They gave her something to eat and let her sleep in the office.

The snow fell and fell, and it was very cold. The people could not put the dog out into the cold. They made her a warm bed in a big box. The dog made friends with everyone. She did not get in anyone's way.

The people liked the dog and let her stay on in the office of the newspaper. And the dog liked her new home very much. But the people did not know what to name their new dog. She was a newspaper dog, and they wanted a newspaper name for her.

Then, one of the people wrote the letters on the machine that newspaper people use. This is how the letters looked—ETAOINSHRDLU.

"Let us take the last six of these letters," said the people, "and give our dog a newspaper name."

That is how this newspaper dog got the name of Shrdlu.

One day the people in the newspaper office found a little puppy in Shrdlu's bed. The people all said Shrdlu had a beautiful baby.

The day after that, the people found not one little puppy, but eight little puppies in Shrdlu's bed. They did not know what to do with so many puppies. They started to think of names for them.

Now the head man in the office did
not like dogs very much. He thought the
people in the newspaper office were all
taking too much time to care for one big
dog and eight little puppies. So he said
they could not keep the dog any longer.
The mother and her puppies had to go.

The other people did not know what
to do. They loved the dogs very much.
They wanted the dogs to have a good
home. So one of them wrote about
Shrdlu and her puppies and put it in the
paper.

When the people in the town read the newspaper, they wanted to see the dogs. So many people came to the newspaper office to see the puppies that the office was full of people all day long.

A picture of Shrdlu and her eight little puppies was put in the newspaper. And, every day, one of the people in the newspaper office wrote something about Shrdlu and her family. The people in the town read about Shrdlu every day.

The man who was head of the office knew that many people were reading his paper. He showed the puppies to everyone. He said nothing about the mother and her puppies having to go.

Shrdlu's Money

Shrdlu and the people in the newspaper office took good care of the puppies. The puppies grew and grew. They ran around the office and got in everyone's way. They barked when people came into the office. Eight puppies can make a lot of noise.

Shrdlu and her puppies ate a lot of food, too. Every day the people at the office put money in a box. Then, one of the people would go to the store and buy food for the dogs. It took a lot of money every day to buy food for Shrdlu and her eight puppies.

Then, the man who was head of the office, and who did not like dogs, said, "A newspaper office is no place to bring up a family of dogs. They eat too much, and they make too much noise. The dogs have to go."

Then, the people at the newspaper office made a place for the puppies in the backyard. All the boys and the girls in the town came to see the puppies. But the puppies barked and made a lot of noise.

One of the people put a box at the door of the newspaper office. Just over the box she wrote:

SHRDLU AND HER PUPPIES
MUST HAVE FOOD.
PUT FOOD MONEY IN THIS BOX.

At once the people put money in the box for Shrdlu and her puppies. The children put in their money. The people at the newspaper office put in some money.

Every day there was a lot of money in the box. There was much more money than they had to have for food. What should be done with all the money?

The people at the office said that Shrdlu should have money in the bank. So they took the money to the bank and put it under Shrdlu's name. More and more money was put in the bank every day.

The man who was head of the newspaper office did not say anything, because everyone in town wanted to know about the newspaper dog who had money in the bank.

Then, one of the men at the office wrote something and put it in the paper. It said:

PLEASE HELP ME

Shrdlu is my name. I am a mother dog with four little boys and four little girls. I cannot think of names for my puppies. Please help me. Send to this newspaper four boys' names and four girls' names for my puppies. And send your name, too. If I give one of my puppies the name you send to me, I will send you a dollar.

Many, many boys' names and girls' names came to the newspaper office. The people had to find the best names. And when the puppies had all been given their names, Shrdlu gave each boy and girl who thought of one of the names a dollar from her bank account.

There was more and more money in the bank for Shrdlu. The people at the office got pretty new collars for the puppies, who were getting big. Every puppy had its own collar with its own name on it. Then, the people took a picture of Shrdlu and her family.

The picture was put in the newspaper, and under the picture it said:

WHO WILL GIVE ONE OF MY PUPPIES A GOOD HOME?

There were many people who wanted one of Shrdlu's puppies. After a time, each little boy puppy and each little girl puppy had a new home. Only Shrdlu was now at the newspaper office.

By this time, many people knew the newspaper that had a dog with the newspaper name of Shrdlu. They knew about Shrdlu's eight puppies and her money in the bank. The head of the newspaper office, who did not like dogs, said that the newspaper office must keep Shrdlu.

Tatters

Five years ago, Ethan was going to have a birthday. And he was going to be five years old. The one thing that Ethan wanted was a dog. He did not want any new toys. He wanted a dog to play with.

Mother and Father thought about getting Ethan a dog.

"We cannot buy a dog," said Mother. "We do not have the money."

"If a dog has no home," said Father, "he is taken to the dog pound. Sometimes there is a dog at the dog pound that would like a good home and that would be a good friend for a little boy."

So Father and Mother and Ethan went to the dog pound. And as soon as Ethan saw Tatters, he fell in love with him.

Tatters was not a very pretty dog.
He did not have much of a tail, and one
ear was hurt. He was black and white
and not very clean. But his big brown
eyes were just asking for someone to love
him. And Ethan loved him as soon as he
saw him.

Later, Ethan was ten years old. And Ethan had a little sister, Carrie, who was three years old. Ethan played with Carrie, but he liked to play with Tatters best of all. Tatters had been the best kind of a family dog. He had looked after Ethan when he started to school. When Carrie came, Tatters loved her very much. He looked after Carrie and watched that nothing hurt her.

One day Father came home and said, "We are going on a vacation. We are going to drive out and see some places that we have never seen before."

Then, what a good time the family had. Mother got their coats and other things. Father and Ethan put good things to eat into a basket. And little Carrie and Tatters ran around the house getting in everyone's way. Tatters did not know what it was all about, but he could tell that the family was very happy.

"We are going to go on a long ride in the car," said Ethan to Tatters. "And you are going with us."

Tatters was very happy when he was in the car with Ethan and Carrie. Father and Mother got into the car, too. Then, the family were off on their vacation.

After a time, they came to a beautiful lake by the road.

"Let us stop here and have something to eat," said Mother. "Then, we can go on and find a place to sleep for the night."

Father stopped the car. He took out the basket. Mother put out the food. And Ethan and Carrie and Tatters thought it was the most fun they had ever had.

After they had eaten, Father said that he thought he would go to sleep under a tree. Mother and Ethan put the things back into the basket. And Carrie and Tatters went off to see what they could find.

Everything was quiet for a time. Then, Tatters started to bark. He barked, and he barked, and he barked.

"Please keep that dog quiet," said Father. "I want to go to sleep. I got tired driving so long."

But Tatters would not stop barking.

"Tatters is only playing with Carrie," said Mother.

"Tatters is playing in a funny way with Carrie," said Ethan. "He is running around and around. And then he will jump at Carrie and push her to the ground."

Father knew that Tatters was trying to take care of Carrie. He jumped to his feet and ran to where Carrie was. Tatters was barking at something in the grass. It was a rattlesnake.

Every time that Carrie started to go to the rattlesnake, Tatters would push her to the ground. And then he went around and around the rattlesnake, barking as hard as he could so that the rattlesnake would watch him and not bite Carrie.

Just as Father got to Carrie, the big rattlesnake bit Tatters.

Father picked up a big stick and killed the rattlesnake.

Father knew that a rattlesnake bite would kill Tatters if they did not get him to a doctor right away.

Mother said, "We must find a doctor for Tatters."

So Father put Tatters and the family into the car. He went as fast as he could to town and found a doctor.

For days, Tatters had to stay with the doctor. But at last, Tatters got well. He is looking after Carrie and Ethan again. And Tatters, the dog that came from the dog pound, is a very happy dog because his family loves him very much.

a
about
account
Adams
Adams'
afraid
after
again
ago
airplane
all
always
am
an
and
another
any
anyone
anyone's
anything
are
arms
around
as
asked
asking
asleep
at
ate
away
baby
back
backdoor
backyard
ball
bank
bark

barked
barking
barn
basket
be
beautiful
because
bed
bedroom
been
before
behind
best
big
bigger
birthday
bit
bite
black
blew
boat
bob
book
both
box
boy
boys
boy's
bread
bring
bringing
brown
bull
Bunco
Bunny
but
buy

by
Byron
Byron's
called
calling
came
can
cannot
car
care
careful
Carrie
carried
carries
carry
carrying
cars
cat
cats
chair
chicken
chickens
children
city
clean
coats
cold
collar
collars
come
coming
corn
could
cows
cried
cry
crying

Curtis
Daddy
dark
day
days
daytime
deep
did
dish
do
dock
doctor
dog
doghouse
dogs
dollar
done
don't
door
doorbell
down
drive
driving
Duke
Duke's
each
ear
eat
eaten
Edward
eight
Ethan
ever
every
everyone
everyone's
everything

eyes
fall
family
far
farm
fast
father
feet
fell
field
fields
find
first
fishing
five
floor
follow
followed
following
food
for
forgot
found
four
friend
friendly
friends
from
front
full
fun
funny
game
gate
gave
get
getting

girl
girls
girl's
give
given
go
going
Golden Queen
gone
good
got
grass
great
green
grew
ground
grow
growing
growl
had
hair
hands
happy
hard
Harry
Harry's
has
have
having
he
head
heard
help
helped
her
here
hill

him
his
hold
home
hooked
horns
horses
house
how
hurt
hurting
I
if
in
into
is
it
its
John
John's
jump
jumped
jumps
just
keep
kill
killed
kind
kitten
knew
know
lady
lake
last
later
laugh
laughed

laughing
lay
leader
learn
learned
leash
leg
legs
let
letter
letters
letting
like
liked
little
live
lived
living
lonesome
long
longer
look
looked
looking
looks
lost
lot
love
loved
loves
machine
made
mail
mailman
make
man
many

maybe
me
men
milk
milked
milking
milkman
money
more
morning
most
mother
Mr.
Mrs.
much
must
my
name
named
names
never
new
newspaper
night
no
noise
nose
not
nothing
now
of
off
office
old
on
once
one

only
onto
open
opened
or
other
our
out
outside
over
own
paper
park
pasture
paws
people
person
pet
picked
picture
place
places
play
played
playing
please
police
pound
pretty
pull
puppies
puppy
puppy's
push
put
putting
queen

Queenie
quiet
radio
ran
rattlesnake
read
reading
red
ride
right
ring
road
room
round
run
running
said
same
sat
saw
say
school
see
seen
send
shall
she
sheep
should
showed
Shrdlu
Shrdlu's
shut
sister
six
sleep
sleeping

sleepy
slipped
small
smell
smelled
smelling
smells
snow
so
some
someone
something
sometimes
somewhere
soon
started
station
stay
stick
stop
stopped
store
street
streets
such
sun
surprise
swim
swimming
tail
take
taken
taking
talked
Tatters
Teddy
Teddy's

teeth	trying
tell	two
ten	under
than	unhappy
thank	up
that	us
the	use
their	vacation
them	very
then	wagged
there	wagging
these	walk
they	walked
thing	walking
things	want
think	wanted
this	war
thought	warm
three	warmed
tie	was
tied	watch
time	watchdog
times	watched
tired	water
to	way
together	we
told	well
Tony	went
Tony's	were
too	wet
took	what
town	when
toys	where
tree	whether
trees	which
tried	while
try	white

who
why
will
wind
window
with
without
woke
woods

work
would
wrote
yard
year
years
yes
you
your